D1064943

ALSO BY ANTHONY DELAUNEY

Owning the Dash: Applying the Mindset of a Fitness Master to the Art of Family Financial Planning

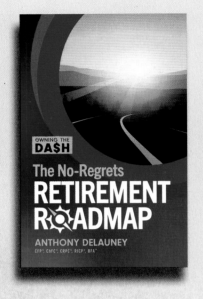

Owning the Dash: The No-Regrets Retirement Roadmap

Dash and Nikki and The Jellybean Game (Book 1 in the Owning the Dash Kids' Book series)

Lilly and May Learn Why Mom and Dad Work (Book 2 in the Owning the Dash Kids' Book series)

To my son, Jason. Thank you for allowing me
to turn our simple game into a wonderful
story that will help families learn (and share)
a valuable life lesson for years to come!

MASCOT
KIDS!
an imprint of Amplify Publishing Group

www.amplifypublishinggroup.com

Rohan and Nyra and Big Sister's Bet

©2023 Anthony C. Delauney. All Rights Reserved. No part of this publication may be reproduced, stored in a retrieval system or transmitted in any form by any means electronic, mechanical, or photocopying, recording or otherwise without the permission of the author.

For more information, please contact:
Mascot Kids, an imprint of Amplify Publishing Group
620 Herndon Parkway, Suite 320
Herndon, VA 20170
info@mascotbooks.com

Library of Congress Control Number: 2022912872

CPSIA Code: PRT0822A
ISBN-13: 978-1-63755-495-1

Printed in the United States

ROHAN AND NYRA
and Big Sister's Bet

Anthony C. Delauney

Illustrated by Chiara Civati

The weekend had arrived. Rohan sat, tapping his feet.
He watched from his window as the cars drove past his street.
He heard a loud horn BEEP. A red car rolled into view.
Rohan burst from his bedroom, and down the stairs he flew.

He rushed to open the front door; as he pulled it back,
a girl came up to him. She was holding a backpack.
"I bet Dad you would be late," Rohan said with a grin.
The girl laughed, then asked, "Are you going to let me in?"
Rohan jumped and wrapped his arms around his big sister.
He did not want to hide just how much he had missed her.

"I have a gift," Nyra said, reaching into her pack.
"I wasn't sure if you wanted it in brown or black."
She tossed Rohan a football and pointed to the yard.
"Want to throw a few?" She winked. "Or is throwing too hard?"

Rohan could not wait. He put on his jacket and shoes.
A challenge from his sister—he would never refuse.

So out the door they went, like so many times before,
but this time was special. Nyra had something in store.
She threw the football to Rohan, who caught it with ease.
He tossed the ball back to her after dodging some trees.

He then danced around Nyra.
  "Is that all that you've got?"
Nyra smirked and shrugged her shoulders.
  "Well, maybe it's not."

"I'll make you a bet," she said, "that Dad once made with me.
I think that you'll like it, but I guess we'll have to see.
Let's keep this game going, and for each catch that you make,
I will give you a dollar, no tricks. It's yours to take.
We can keep playing until you say you want to stop,
but if at any point the football happens to drop,
then all the money is lost, and the game will be done.
So, what do you think, Rohan? Does this challenge sound fun?"

Rohan leapt into the sky. "This game will be easy!"
He did his touchdown dance, which looked completely cheesy.
Then he glanced at his wrist with a glimmer in his eye.
A new toy watch was exactly what he hoped to buy.

Nyra passed the football. Rohan caught it with both hands.
He cheered and pointed to his imaginary fans.
"That's one dollar," Nyra said. She signaled for the ball.
She then threw a few more passes. Rohan caught them all.

After each pass, Rohan counted the money he'd won.
Five dollars. Then ten dollars. Nyra asked, "Are we done?"
Rohan laughed. He imagined other things he could buy.
Video games, some candy, or a plane he could fly.

"Let's throw some more," he said as he got himself ready.
Nyra did as he asked. Each pass came nice and steady.

Fifteen dollars! Then twenty dollars! Then twenty-five!
Rohan wondered how long he could keep his streak alive.
His hands had started to sweat, and his legs were tired too.
One more catch to buy the watch. That's all he had to do.

So, he looked at his big sister. "Let's try for one more."
Nyra did as she was asked and let the football soar.
Rohan caught the ball again. He stood beaming with joy.
He had what he needed to buy his favorite toy.

But as he tossed the ball back, a thought popped in his head.
What could I buy with more money? is what the thought said.

He dreamt of even bigger prizes that he could get.

A remote-control car, or a supersonic jet!

He pondered. *I can handle a few more easy throws.*

Nyra asked, "Are we done?" What do you think Rohan chose?

He stared at the football and wiped the sweat from his face.

He signaled for the ball as he set his feet in place.

Nyra threw it as straight and as steady as she could.

It glided through the air in a spiral that looked good.

Rohan reached out as the football sailed into his chest.

It fumbled between his arms, and you can guess the rest.

Rohan paused in disbelief. All he could do was stare.
Knowing what had happened was a truth he couldn't bear.
He looked up at his sister and then back at the ball.
He thought of all the money. He had just lost it all.

Why, he asked himself, *why did I ask for another?*
Nyra stayed silent. She moved closer to her brother.
"I was doing so well," Rohan cried, clenching his fist,
"but I wanted even more. Why couldn't I resist?"

"I know how you feel," Nyra said. "I dropped the ball too.
Dad played this game with me when I was as young as you.
I remember throwing a fit. I got so upset.
But now it's a life lesson I will never forget."

Nyra placed her left hand on top of her brother's head.
She rustled through Rohan's hair, and then she softly said,
"Life is full of choices that we often have to make
so when you make a choice, remember what is at stake.
Sometimes we get greedy, and we gamble what we've got.
The next time you get tempted, don't throw away your shot."

"I understand," Rohan said, after thinking a while.
He looked over at Nyra and gave a gentle smile.
Then he hopped up to his feet, and he brushed off his knee.
"So, what do you think, big sister, best two out of three?"

Nyra belted out a laugh. "Maybe another day.
It looks like Mom and Dad are coming out now to play."
Rohan picked up the football. He thanked Nyra again.
"I love having a sister who's also my best friend!"

ABOUT THE AUTHOR

Anthony C. Delauney is a financial advisor based in Raleigh, North Carolina, who has a passion for helping families. He is the founder of Owning the Dash, LLC, an organization dedicated to helping educate and inspire families as they work to achieve their financial goals. His other books include *Owning the Dash: Applying the Mindset of a Fitness Master to the Art of Family Financial Planning*, *Owning the Dash: The No-Regrets Retirement Roadmap*, *Dash and Nikki and The Jellybean Game*, and *Lilly and May Learn Why Mom and Dad Work*.

Rohan and Nyra and Big Sister's Bet is Anthony's third book in the Owning the Dash Kids' Book series. With the help of his wife Laura, daughter Abbie, and son Jason, Anthony wrote this book to entertain children of all ages and to teach them an important financial lesson that will help guide them in the years to come. Many more fun adventures await all the children in the Owning the Dash Kids' Book series! Anthony, Laura, Abbie, and Jason hope you enjoy the book!

Special thanks to the Patel family! I'm grateful for your support in this journey. Aarna, the Owning the Dash Kids Book series would not be the same without you.